WEATHER MAPS

Ian F. Mahaney

The Rosen Publishing Group's

PowerKids Press™

New York

To my parents, who still deal with me daily

Published in 2007 by The Rosen Publishing Group, Inc.
29 East 21st Street, New York, NY 10010

First Edition

Editor: Jennifer Way
Book Design: Greg Tucker
Photo Researcher: Jeffrey Wendt

Photo Credits: Cover, pp. 1, 5, 9, 10 Greg Tucker adapted from NASA/JPL-Caltech; cover (left) © Royalty-Free/Corbis; p. 6 NOAA/NWS;
pp. 13, 14, 17 Library of Congress Geography and Map Division; p. 18 © Getty Images; p. 21 Image Science and Analysis Laboratory,
NASA-Johnson Space Center.

Library of Congress Cataloging-in-Publication Data

Mahaney, Ian F.
  Weather maps / Ian F. Mahaney.— 1st ed.
      p. cm. — (Map it!)
  Includes index.
  ISBN 1-4042-3057-2 (library binding) — ISBN 1-4042-2213-8 (pbk.) — ISBN 1-4042-2403-3 (six pack)
  1. Map reading—Juvenile literature. 2. Weather—Juvenile literature. I. Title. II. Series.

GA130.M367 2007
551.6022'3—dc22

                                    2005032939

Manufactured in the United States of America

Contents

Maps are everywhere and they help us understand the world in which we live. They help us travel through unfamiliar areas. They help us understand news and events throughout the world. Do you know the correct way to use a map? Have you wondered what a map really is?

A map is a picture of an area on Earth. Maps can even be pictures of the entire world. Most maps have a **legend**. The legend shows you how to read the **information** on the map. On a weather map, the legend tells you what the different colors, **symbols**, and lines on the map mean. This book will teach you how to read and understand a weather map.

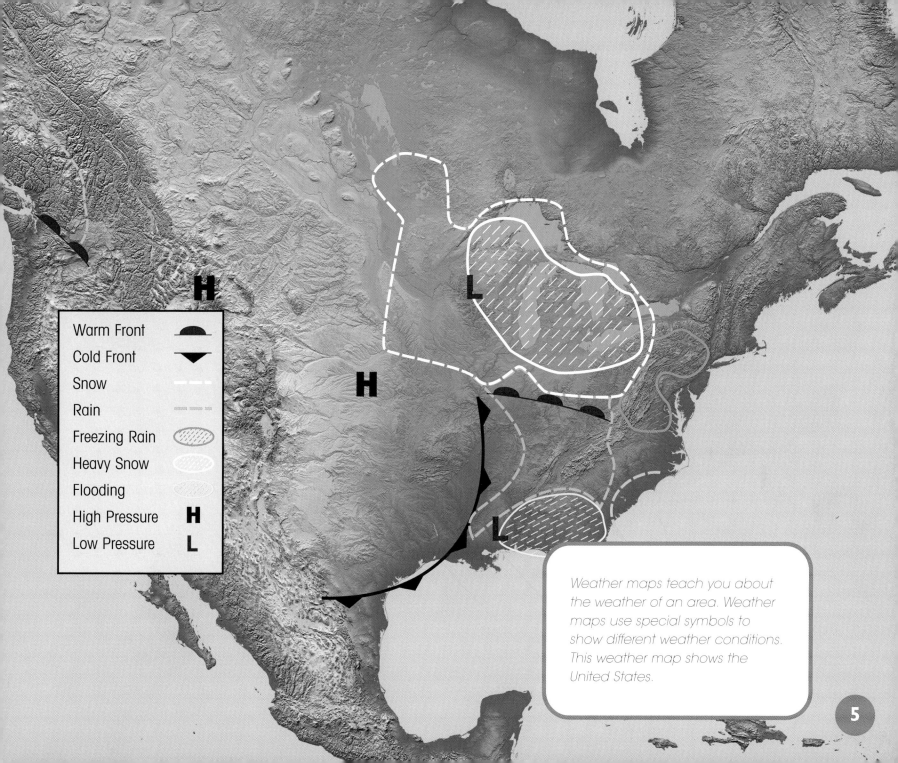

Warm Front	⬖
Cold Front	▼
Snow	– – –
Rain	— — —
Freezing Rain	⬭
Heavy Snow	⬭
Flooding	⬭
High Pressure	**H**
Low Pressure	**L**

Weather maps teach you about the weather of an area. Weather maps use special symbols to show different weather conditions. This weather map shows the United States.

5

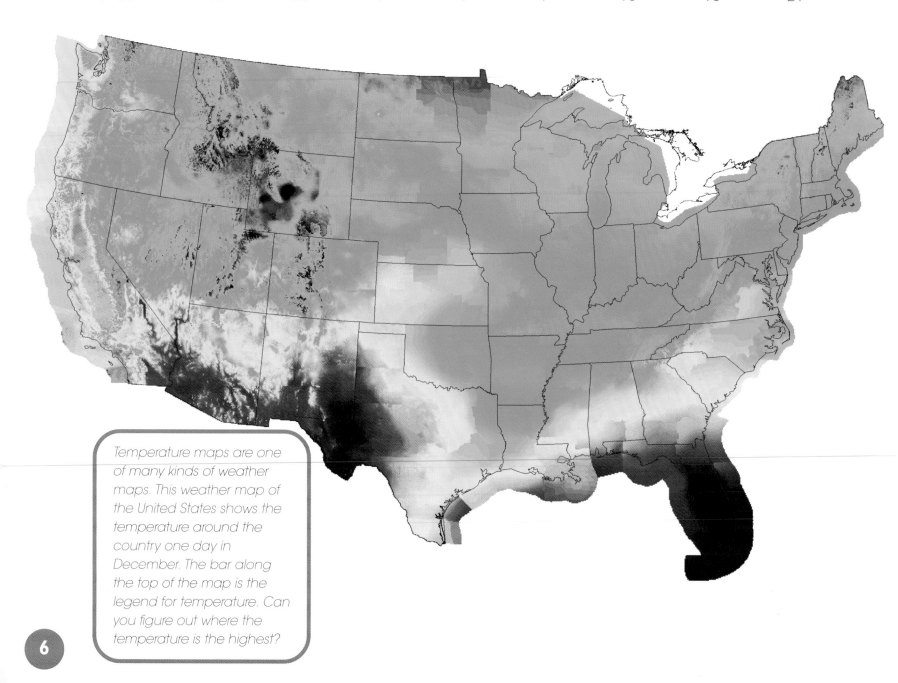

°F -10 0 10 20 30 40 50 60 70
°C -23 -18 -12 -7 -1 4 10 16 21

Temperature maps are one of many kinds of weather maps. This weather map of the United States shows the temperature around the country one day in December. The bar along the top of the map is the legend for temperature. Can you figure out where the temperature is the highest?

What Is Weather?

Weather is a combination of things that happen in the **atmosphere** above Earth. These are heat, wind, **air pressure**, and moisture. The Sun has an effect on these things, which in turn causes changes in the weather. **Precipitation**, wind, and heat waves are examples of weather.

Although it may not seem like it, air has weight, air moves, and air has moisture. The weight of the air is called air pressure. Air pressure changes depending on many things. For example, hot air weighs more than cold air. Air also moves. Warm air rises and cooler air falls. This **circulation** of air causes wind. Air also contains moisture. This moisture can collect in the form of clouds or fog. It can also fall in different forms of precipitation. The combination of wind, pressure, heat, and moisture in the air creates different weather in different areas at different times.

What Is a Weather Map?

Maps give you information about an area. A weather map explains what type of weather to expect in the area the map shows. This is called **forecasting**. For example, a weather map can show you what **temperature** or what type of precipitation is expected in different areas. A weather map can also show whether cloud cover or changes in air pressure are forecasted.

A weather map shows these weather patterns using symbols. Temperature is usually shown with colors. A weather map also includes symbols for different types of precipitation and for air pressure.

Weather maps can be used to describe the current weather in an area such as a city, a state, or a country. Weather maps sometimes also include charts that list the **accumulated** precipitation in an area. Sometimes they even include historical weather records.

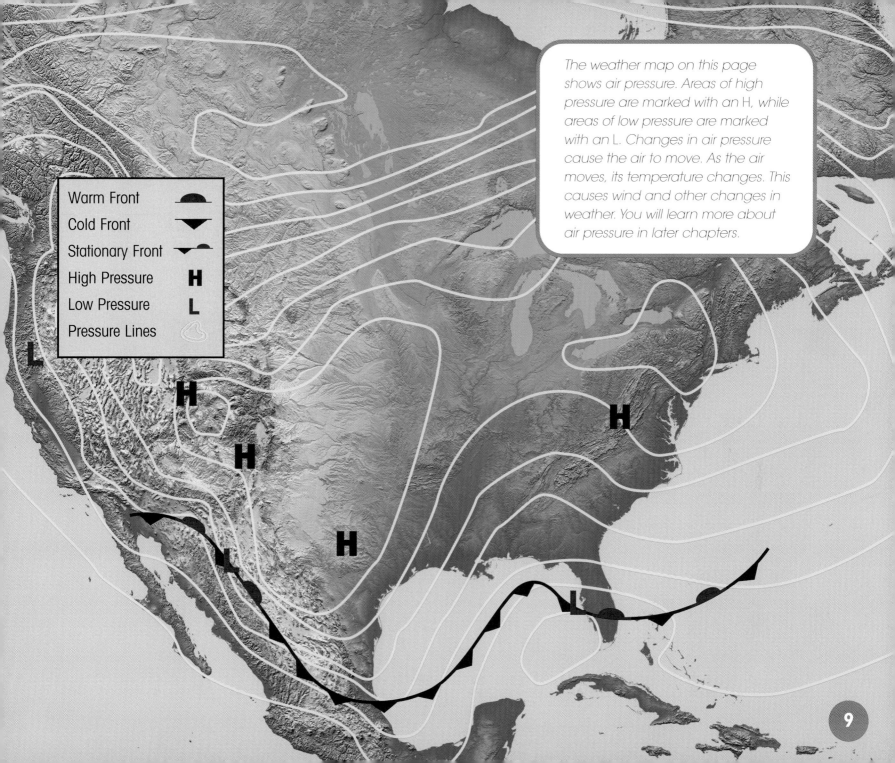

Warm Front

Cold Front

Stationary Front

High Pressure   **H**

Low Pressure   **L**

Pressure Lines

The weather map on this page shows air pressure. Areas of high pressure are marked with an H, while areas of low pressure are marked with an L. Changes in air pressure cause the air to move. As the air moves, its temperature changes. This causes wind and other changes in weather. You will learn more about air pressure in later chapters.

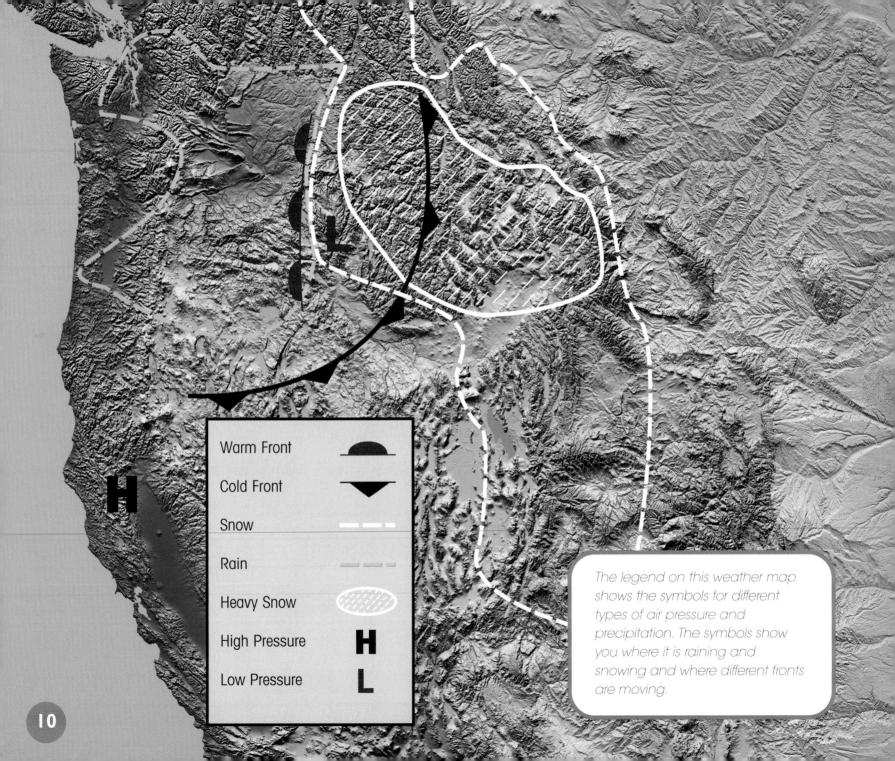

Warm Front

Cold Front

Snow

Rain

Heavy Snow

High Pressure **H**

Low Pressure **L**

The legend on this weather map shows the symbols for different types of air pressure and precipitation. The symbols show you where it is raining and snowing and where different fronts are moving.

Symbols on a Weather Map

It is important to understand the symbols used on weather maps. Look at the weather map on the left. On the map you will find symbols, such as shapes, lines, and colors. Below the map you will find a legend that explains these symbols.

Temperature is usually color coded on a weather map. For example, the map on the left shows that places where the forecast calls for cold weather are blue. The areas where it will be hot are red. Weather maps also have symbols that stand for other kinds of weather. The legend also has symbols that tell you what type of major weather changes are on the way. These are known as warm fronts and cold fronts. Look at the map on the left. Can you tell where the forecast calls for snow?

Weather maps can show the forecast, but they can also center on one part of weather. For example, a weather map can center on temperature. Temperature is measured in **degrees** Fahrenheit and degrees Celsius. The United States uses the Fahrenheit scale. Scientists and most other nations use the Celsius scale.

A temperature map may show the forecasted temperature for a certain day. This kind of temperature map can help you be ready for that day's weather. Other temperature maps may show the average temperature range for a period of time. This kind of temperature map can help you understand what the weather is usually like and if the forecast for that day is calling for unusual weather. Look at the two temperature maps on the left. They show the average temperatures in January and August.

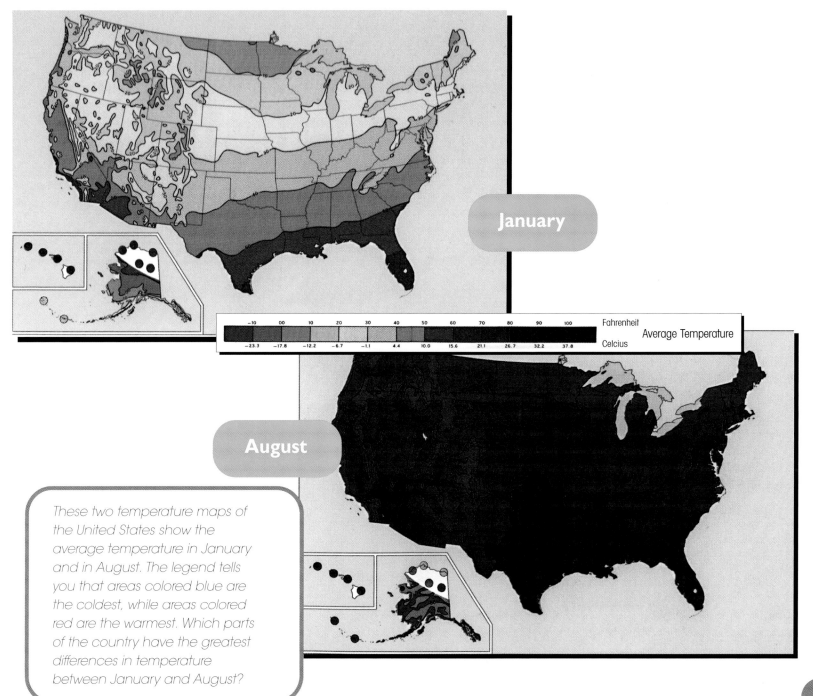

January

August

Fahrenheit

| −10 | 00 | 10 | 20 | 30 | 40 | 50 | 60 | 70 | 80 | 90 | 100 |

Average Temperature

Celcius

| −23.3 | −17.8 | −12.2 | −6.7 | −1.1 | 4.4 | 10.0 | 15.6 | 21.1 | 26.7 | 32.2 | 37.8 |

These two temperature maps of the United States show the average temperature in January and in August. The legend tells you that areas colored blue are the coldest, while areas colored red are the warmest. Which parts of the country have the greatest differences in temperature between January and August?

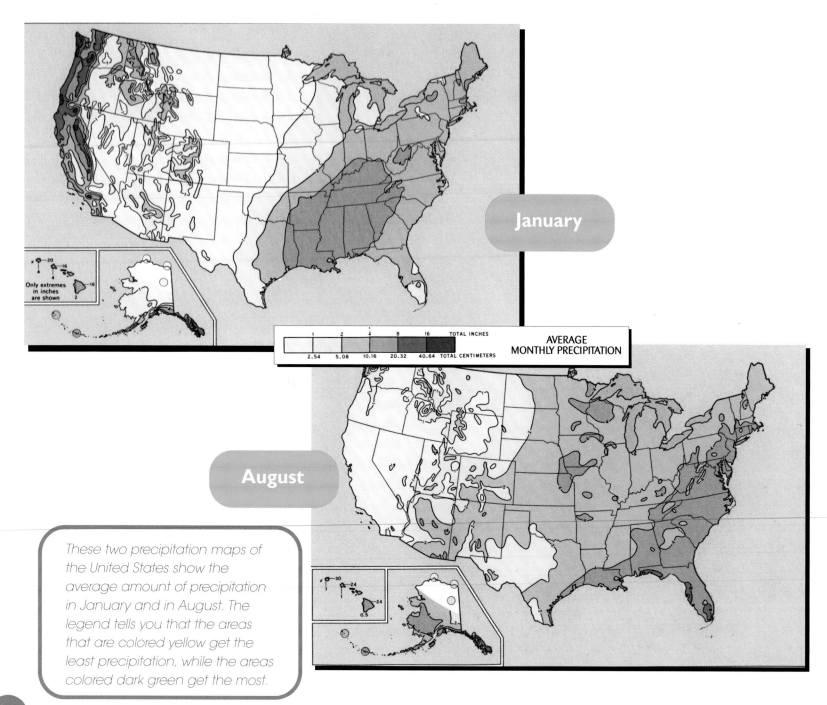

January

August

TOTAL INCHES

	1	2	4	8	16
2.54	5.08	10.16	20.32	40.64	TOTAL CENTIMETERS

AVERAGE MONTHLY PRECIPITATION

Only extremes in inches are shown

These two precipitation maps of the United States show the average amount of precipitation in January and in August. The legend tells you that the areas that are colored yellow get the least precipitation, while the areas colored dark green get the most.

14

Some weather maps show precipitation and air pressure. Precipitation maps use different symbols in the legend to show different kinds of precipitation on the map. For example, snow might be shown by snowflakes, and rain may look like dots. Other precipitation maps use letters to show precipitation. For example, **R** may stand for rain, and **SN** may stand for snow.

An air pressure map can be harder to read. Some air pressure maps use the symbols **H** and **L** to show areas of high and low pressure. Other air pressure maps use **isobars**. An isobar is a line drawn on the weather map that connects areas of like pressure. The closer an isobar is to the low-pressure area, the lower the pressure. The closer an isobar is to the high-pressure area, the higher the air pressure.

Knowing the four basic directions is an important part of understanding all maps, including weather maps. If you look at the map on the left, you will see that a **compass rose** is marked with an N on the top, an S on the bottom, an E on the right, and a W on the left. These stand for the four main directions, which are north, south, east, and west.

Understanding directions will help you understand wind as a part of weather. The wind blows in a direction. For example, a west wind blows from the west toward the east. If you were to trace the direction of a west wind on the map with your finger, it would move from the left to the right. Looking at the map on the left page, can you figure out which way the wind is blowing?

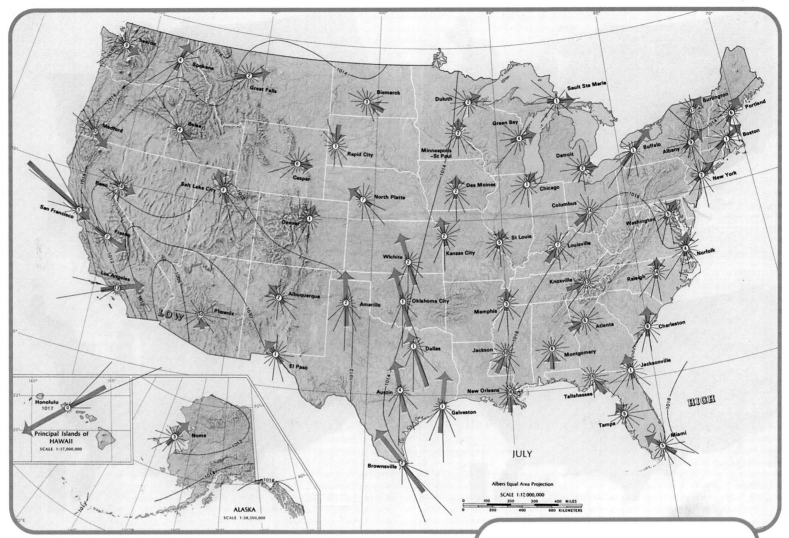

JULY

Albers Equal Area Projection
SCALE 1:17,000,000

AVERAGE MONTHLY WINDS

MILES
PER HOUR

This weather map shows wind speed and wind direction. The legend tells you that the shape at the end, called a barb, tells you the direction from which the wind is coming. The lines connected to the barbs tell you how fast the wind is blowing. Wind is measured in miles and kilometers per hour.

17

DBZ

75
70
65
60
55
50
45
40
35
30
25
20
15
10
5
ND

+ Danville   + Kerr Lake

+ Roanoke Rapids

+ Elizabeth City

+ Durham   + Rocky Mount
+ Raleigh   + Williamston   Columbia

                          + Greenville
Goldsboro
            Kinston   Cape Hatteras
Fayetteville   New Bern
        Clinton
    + Kenansville
              Jacksonville

+ Lumberton   Morehead City

        Wilmington

Meteorologists use radar to look at
precipitation. Weather radar works by
sending beams into the air. How much of
that beam and how fast the beam reflects
back is then measured. Radar beams reflect
back from different types of precipitation at
different speeds. Radar beams reflect back
from heavy precipitation differently, too. This is
a radar picture of a hurricane off the coast
of North Carolina. A hurricane is a large
storm with heavy rain and strong winds.

State Line ——————
County Line ——————
City   +
Freeway ——————

Forecasting Weather

Meteorology is the study of weather. Meteorologists study weather and also forecast the weather. They make forecasts based on some of the ideas that we have talked about in the past chapters. Meteorologists also use tools to help them make weather forecasts. The most important of these tools is the **barometer**. A barometer measures air pressure. Studying changes in barometric pressure and studying changes in the wind direction give meteorologists an idea of what type of weather to expect within the next day.

To make a more long-range forecast, meteorologists use the fact that weather generally travels from west to east in the United States. For example, if it is raining in Ohio, the rain will usually move east toward Pennsylvania. Meteorologists also use radar and **satellites** to look at how weather is moving and to make weather maps.

How Weather Maps Are Made

There are thousands of weather stations around the world. These are places where information about weather is collected. Weather stations can be found on special balloons, ships, airplanes, and buildings. Information from weather stations can include barometer readings, temperature, accumulated precipitation, cloud cover, wind direction, and **humidity**. Humidity is a measure of the amount of water present in the air. Meteorologists use the information from weather stations to help forecast the weather.

Satellites are other tools used in collecting weather information and making weather maps. Satellites take pictures of the weather as it appears from space. Satellites help in tracking storms, such as hurricanes. Weather maps are made from the pictures satellites take. Meteorologists are better able to forecast the path of storms and to warn people before they arrive by using these maps.

Meteorologists also use satellites to follow weather. Satellites take pictures of Earth from outer space. Meteorologists can look at cloud cover and watch how weather changes as it moves around Earth by using satellite pictures. This is a satellite picture of a hurricane in the Gulf of Mexico.

Now that you know more about weather maps, do you know where you can find them? Weather maps can be found in places that are updated often, such as newspapers or the Internet. They are also on the TV news. Newspaper weather maps usually include temperature ranges and precipitation data from all over the country, as well as historical record weather for that day. Most TV news shows have a weather forecast that uses weather maps.

All these places use weather maps to forecast the weather. The meteorologists who create these forecasts use their knowledge of weather and weather maps to make the most correct forecasts they can. The growing use of satellites to create weather maps has made weather mapping more exact for more long-range forecasting. Now that you know how to read and understand weather maps, you can use what you have learned to follow the weather all over the world.

Glossary

accumulated (uh-KYOO-myuh-layt-ed) Built up.

air pressure (EHR PREH-shur) The weight of the air.

atmosphere (AT-muh-sfeer) The layer of gases around an object in space. On Earth this layer is air.

barometer (buh-RAH-meh-tur) A tool used to measure air pressure, or the weight of air.

circulation (ser-kyuh-LAY-shun) A form of movement from person to person, or from place to place.

compass rose (KUM-pus ROHZ) A drawing on a map that shows directions.

degrees (dih-GREEZ) The way in which temperature is measured.

forecasting (FOR-kast-ing) Figuring out when something will happen.

humidity (hyoo-MIH-dih-tee) The amount of moisture in the air.

information (in-fer-MAY-shun) Knowledge or facts.

isobars (EYE-suh-barz) Lines on a weather map that show areas of air pressure.

legend (LEH-jend) A box on a map that tells what the figures on the map mean.

meteorology (mee-tee-uh-RAH-luh-jee) The study of the weather.

precipitation (preh-sih-pih-TAY-shun) Any moisture that falls from the sky. Rain and snow are precipitation.

satellites (SA-tih-lyts) Machines in space that circle Earth and that are used to track weather.

symbols (SIM-bulz) Objects or pictures that stand for something else.

temperature (TEM-pur-cher) How hot or cold something is.

Index

A
air pressure, 7–8, 15, 19
atmosphere, 7

B
barometer, 19–20

C
cold fronts, 11
compass rose, 16

F
forecasting, 8, 11–12,
    19–20, 22

H
humidity, 20

I
isobar(s), 15

L
legend, 4, 11, 15

M
meteorologists, 20, 22
meteorology, 19

P
precipitation, 7–8, 15, 20, 22

S
satellites, 19–20, 22
symbols, 4, 8, 11, 15

T
temperature, 8, 12, 20, 22

W
warm fronts, 11
weather stations, 20
wind, 7, 16, 19–20

Web Sites

Due to the changing nature of Internet links, PowerKids Press has developed an online list of Web sites related to the subject of this book. This site is updated regularly. Please use this link to access the list:

www.powerkidslinks.com/mapit/weather/